Mallory's Guide to Boys, Brothers, Dads, and Dogs

For Becca and Adam
Love, Mommy

For my husband Josh, my brother Phillip,
my dad Alan, and my dog Shadow
—J.K.

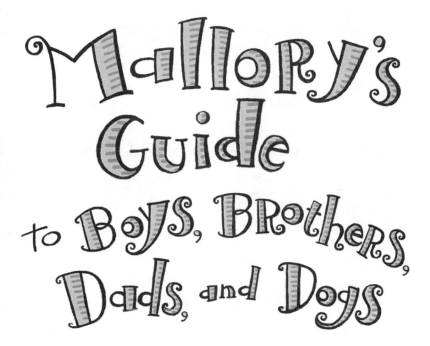

Mallory's Guide
to Boys, Brothers, Dads, and Dogs

by Laurie Friedman
illustrations by Jennifer Kalis

MINNEAPOLIS

CONTENTS

A WORD FROM MALLORY

My name is Mallory McDonald, like the restaurant but no relation, age just turned ten, and I have a problem. Actually, I have four of them and they're all male (I'm not talking about the kind the postman delivers).

If you're wondering just what these problems are, I'll tell you.

Problem #1: The boy that I like doesn't like me back.

He might if he knew I existed, but he doesn't even know my name.

Here's the good news: I know his. It's JT (which stands for Justin Trent but should stand for *Just Terrific*).

Problem #2: My brother is mad at me. He thinks it's "ridiculous" that I like someone in his grade. He says I need to stick to boys my own age. I say he should stick to M.H.O.B. (Short for *minding his own business.*)

Problem #3: My dad is upset about my grades.

I made a bad grade on a math test, and Dad says I'm spending too much time thinking about Mallory + JT when I should be thinking about the addition in my textbook.

Problem #4: My brother's dog stinks!

You're probably wondering why this is my problem when it's not even my dog, but here's why it is:

Max (that's my brother, not the dog) has been playing a lot of baseball lately, and since he's never home, Champ (that's his dog) likes to hang out in my room on my bed. Now my bed smells just like my brother's dog.

I may not be a math whiz, but I know this much: I've got lots of problems, and starting tomorrow, I'm going to start looking for some solutions.

OPERATION: GET NOTICED

Striped leggings.

Check.

Plaid tunic top. Green headband.

Check. Check.

Purple Nails. Yellow rain boots. Sparkly sunglasses.

Check. Check. Check.

I look in the bathroom mirror and smile at my reflection. "If this doesn't get me

noticed, I don't know what will," I say to
my cat.

Cheeseburger purrs like she approves.
I rub her head. "Wish me luck," I say.
When I walk into the kitchen, Mom, Dad,
and Max are already there. I don't say a
word. I want to see if they notice me and
they do.

"Mallory, did you forget to look in
the mirror when you got dressed this

morning?" Max gags like the sight of me is enough to make him sick.

Not exactly the reaction I had hoped for, but my brother doesn't know the first thing about fashion.

Dad looks up from his newspaper and smiles. "Mallory, you're looking bright and cheery this morning."

Max laughs. "I don't know about cheery but definitely bright."

Mom puts her coffee cup down on the counter and comes over to where I'm standing. "Sweet Potato, your outfit is a little bright this morning. Maybe you want to take off the boots." Mom plucks the glasses off my face. "And I don't think you need these for school."

I take the glasses back from Mom, put them back on, and grab a banana out of the bowl on the counter. I take a bite.

"I'm glad you all noticed my outfit," I say when I'm done chewing.

I finish my banana, but I don't tell my family why I'm glad they noticed. There's only one person I'm telling that to, and I can't wait another minute to see her. "Got to go," I say. I dump my peel in the trash and head next door.

My best friend, Mary Ann, is already outside waiting for me.

"Stop! Stop! Stop!" says Mary Ann when she sees me. She holds up her hand like she's a traffic cop. "Where do you think you're going like that?"

I link my arm through hers. "C'mon. I'll tell you on the way to school."

I look around before I start talking. "Where are Joey and Winnie?" I ask quietly.

Mary Ann frowns like she doesn't get what's going on and she's not sure she likes it. "They're finishing breakfast. Why are you whispering?"

I look behind me before I answer her question.

I have to make sure my brother and Joey and Winnie are nowhere near me before I tell Mary Ann my big news. "I have a crush," I say in my quietest voice.

Mary Ann still looks confused. "If you have a crush, why are you wearing that weird outfit?"

I push my glasses up on the bridge of my nose. I don't see how Mary Ann can be talking about clothes when I just told her one of the biggest, most important secrets of my life. "Don't you want to know who I have a crush on?" I ask.

"Of course I do," says Mary Ann. "But I also want to know why you're wearing that outfit."

I put my mouth close to her ear. Even though no one else is near us, I'm not taking any chances. "I have a crush on JT in sixth grade, and I'm wearing these clothes so he'll notice me."

Mary Ann gives me a *the-first-part-of-what-you-said-makes-total-sense-because-JT-is-cute-but-I-don't-get-the-second-part-at-all* look.

I keep explaining. "At lunch, I'm planning to walk by the sixth-grade table. When JT notices what I'm wearing, he'll stop eating and start talking to me. It's called *Operation: Get Noticed*." I smile like I'm proud of my plan.

But Mary Ann doesn't smile back. "I'm not sure that's a good idea," she says as we walk through the gates of Fern Falls Elementary.

Even if Mary Ann isn't sure about my plan, I am. "Don't worry," I tell my friend. I take off my glasses and slip them into my pocket for later. *"Operation: Get Noticed* is going to be a big success."

The only hard part is going to be waiting for lunch. I try to listen while my teacher, Mr. Knight, talks about fractions and decimal points. It's almost impossible to pay attention to math when my brain is busy thinking about my plan.

I've gone over it in my head a million times.

I'm going to get in line and get a tray of food. I'll make sure I know exactly where JT is sitting. I'll walk past his table. When he sees me, he's going to say, "Hey, you in the glasses, I'm JT. What's your name?" I'll tell him my name, and then we'll eat lunch together. When we're done, he'll take my tray and dump my leftovers in the trash. Then he'll do something cute like call me Glasses Girl, and we'll eat lunch together every day after that.

Just thinking about it makes me smile.

"Mallory, I'm waiting." I hear my name and lots of giggles.

When I look up, everyone in my class is looking at me and so is my teacher. "Mallory, can you please give me the answer."

Maybe I could if I knew what page we're on or which problem we're doing, but I have no idea. I start flipping through my math book. I can feel my face turning red.

Mr. Knight waits a few seconds, and then he calls on Arielle, who answers the question. He looks at her like he's pleased, and then he looks at me like he's not. "Mallory, please pay attention."

I nod like that's exactly what I'm planning to do, but it isn't easy. The hands on the clock seem like someone stuck them down with gum. When the lunch bell finally rings, I grab Mary Ann's arm.

When we get to the cafeteria, it's already filled with kids.

The first, second, and third graders are sitting down at their tables. Some fourth and fifth graders are in line. I see JT sitting at a table with a bunch of sixth-grade girls and boys, including my brother. I wish Max wasn't there, but if I ignore him, he'll probably ignore me.

"C'mon," I say to Mary Ann. I take a tray and hand one to Mary Ann.

Mary Ann puts a slice of pizza on her tray. "Mallory, I don't think you should go through with your plan." She gives me an *I-have-a-boyfriend-so-I'm-an-expert-on-how-to-*

get-a-boyfriend look. "When I first started to like C-Lo, I didn't do anything special to get his attention. I don't think you need to do anything special to get JT's attention."

I take a plate of chicken fingers and french fries. Maybe my friend doesn't like my plan, but I do. I know it's going to work. I take an apple and a bowl of chocolate pudding.

I pull my sunglasses out of my pocket and put them on. "Time to put *Operation: Get Noticed* into action," I tell Mary Ann.

I start to walk across the cafeteria. I keep my eyes on JT as I pass a table of second-grade boys. JT is sitting at his table, eating a sandwich. So far, so good.

I pass a table of fifth-grade girls. JT is drinking fruit punch. At least, I think it's fruit punch. It's a little hard to tell what he's drinking with these glasses on. So far, still good.

Only two more tables before I get to JT's table.

I pass first-grade girls. I try not to speed up. I don't want to look like I'm in a hurry to pass JT's table. JT and his friends are laughing about something, but it's hard to tell what it is.

I walk past a table of third-grade boys. I can hear JT and his friends laughing like something is really funny. It's probably the chicken fingers. Someone probably made a joke that they taste more like fingers than chicken.

I cross my toes as I get closer to his table. Even though it's hard to walk with crossed toes, rain boots, and sunglasses, I do it anyway.

I slow down as I start to pass his table. I want to make sure I give him plenty of time to notice me. But JT isn't the one who notices.

"Hey," says a boy as I pass their table. "Is today Halloween?"

"Where did you get your costume?" a girl asks me.

Another boy points to my glasses. "Is it sunny in here?"

"It must be raining," says another girl. "Check out her boots."

I can hear everyone at JT's table laughing, and I don't think it's at the

chicken fingers. This wasn't supposed
to happen. I look at Max. I give him an
I-could-use-some-big-brotherly-help-here
look, but Max doesn't look like he is in a
helping mood.

He looks like he's in a mad mood.

I look down at my rain boots, but when
I do, something else happens that wasn't
supposed to.

I trip and drop my tray.

Chicken fingers and french fries scatter
all over the cafeteria floor.

My apple rolls under a table.

My sunglasses fall off my face.

My yellow rain boots are covered in
chocolate pudding.

Now everyone at JT's table is really
laughing, and I know it's not at the chicken
fingers. Everyone in the cafeteria is looking
at one thing, and that one thing is me.

I see the cafeteria lady coming toward me with a mop and a broom.

I grab my sunglasses and put them back on my face. Even though the glasses make it harder for me to see, they don't make it harder for me to hear. Everyone is still laughing.

I try not to look at the mess all over the
floor of the cafeteria, but it is all I can see.

This was not how *Operation: Get Noticed*
was supposed to go down.

PLAN B

My first plan didn't go so well. But I take a deep breath and try to stay positive. *Plan B Is for Brother* will be a big success.

"Mallory, do you want to crack the eggs?" asks Mom.

I pick up an egg and tap it against the side of the mixing bowl. Mom knows that when we bake cookies, I like breaking the eggs into the batter.

While the mixer swirls the eggs into the

butter and sugar, I close my eyes and go over my plan.

Max will come home from baseball practice. He'll see the cookies I spent all morning baking for him. He'll eat one and realize I'm a good baker. He'll eat another one, notice the extra nuts I put in just for him, and realize I'm a good sister. He'll eat another one and decide it's silly to stay mad at me because of what happened in the cafeteria at school this week. He'll eat one more, and when I ask him if he'll talk to JT about liking me, Max will say, "Sure. No problem." Then JT will like me, and I'll live happily ever after, just like they do in fairy tales.

"Time to add the flour and vanilla," says Mom.

I pour while Mom stirs. "Thanks again for helping me bake," I tell Mom.

She smiles. "I'm happy to see that you want to do something nice for your brother."

I smile back, but I don't say anything
like why I'm doing something nice for
my brother. Even though Mom works at
my school, I don't think she heard what
happened in the cafeteria, and if she did,
she isn't making a big deal out of it.

Max is the only one who is doing that.
He's been mad at me all week. He says,

"You embarrassed yourself and me too by trying to get JT's attention."

He told me it's bad enough having a younger sister at the same school, but it's even worse that I like someone in his grade. He said I should stick to boys my own age.

I don't know who put him in charge of deciding who I can and can't like. But I do know I need to get back on his good side. I could use his help right now.

"We're ready for the chocolate chips and nuts," says Mom.

I empty the package of chocolate chips into the mixing bowl. I pour in the extra-big bowl of nuts that I broke into little, tiny pieces myself.

Mom stirs everything together. I spoon little drops of dough onto the cookie sheets, and Mom puts the cookies in the oven.

Now all I have to do is to wait for them to bake and for Max to come home.

While I'm waiting, I sit down at the computer in the kitchen and click on my email. My inbox is empty, so I start on an email.

Subject: *Plan B* Update
From: malgal
To: chatterbox

Mary Ann,

I know you think *Plan B* will NOT work, but that is because you don't think anything will work when it has to do with Max. But DON'T worry. It WILL work. Max LOVES cookies! His stomach LOVES cookies! Once he EATS the cookies I baked, he will do WHATEVER I ask him to do. I just know it. I.W.W.M.L.O.M.P.H.W. (Short for: *I will*

write more later once my plan has worked.)
Stay tuned!
Mallory

The buzzer goes off on the oven, and I help Mom take the cookies out.

When the door slams a few minutes later, I jump. Time to put *Plan B* into action. I grab a plate and fill it with cookies. I run to meet Max at the door.

"Want a cookie?" I ask.

Max drops his baseball bag, grabs a cookie, and shoves in into his mouth.

He doesn't say anything, but I can tell he likes them. He's always hungry after practice. "How about some more?" I ask.

Max takes a big handful of cookies.

"I made them especially for you," I tell my brother.

"Thanks," he mumbles even though his mouth is full.

I know now is my chance to talk while Max has a mouthful of cookies.

I take a deep breath and get started. "Max, I know you're still mad at me about what happened in the cafeteria the other day. I'm really sorry about that. I made these cookies with extra nuts just for you, and I promise not to do anything like that again. But here's the problem: I like JT and he doesn't like me back because he doesn't know me. Since you're in his grade and you know him, maybe you can tell him to like me and then he will."

I stop and wait for Max to say something like, *"Sure, no problem and thanks for the cookies."* But that's not what he says.

"Mallory, I told you to stick to boys your own age."

I tap my foot like that wasn't the answer I was looking for and I'm waiting for Max to say something else, and he does.

"JT knows who you are. Everyone in the school knows who you are after that stunt in the cafeteria."

That was NOT what I wanted to hear.

I look down at the plate in my hands. *Plan B* isn't going as well as I'd hoped it would. There are only three cookies left.

Max takes two. "Anyway, JT already has a girlfriend."

This was definitely NOT what I wanted to hear. I can't believe he has a girlfriend.

Max takes the last cookie and pops it into his mouth. "Thanks for the cookies," he says when he's done chewing. He starts to walk down the hall, but I stop him. I didn't spend the morning baking for nothing.

"I didn't know JT has a girlfriend."

"Yeah. Bailey." Max says her name like it's old news.

But it's not old news to me. "Bailey, Winnie's best friend, Bailey? Bailey, long, blonde hair and big, blue eyes, Bailey?"

Max nods like that's the one, then walks down the hall.

I watch Max walk away. Then I go to my room.

When I get there, Max's dog, Champ, is asleep on my bed next to Cheeseburger. I hold my nose. My room smells like a dirty dog.

Ever since baseball season started, Champ has been spending a *lot* of time in my room and Max has been spending *no* time taking care of him. "Hey Max, come get your dog and give him a bath," I shout down the hall.

"Champ doesn't need a bath," Max shouts back.

I don't know which is worse. A smelly dog or a brother who won't help me when I need him to. I plop down on the bed between Champ and Cheeseburger.

Plan B Is for Brother definitely did not go according to plan.

FACING THE FACTS

Mr. Knight walks around the circle of desks.

Anderson. Brooks. Lopez. Martin.

All these names can be added to the list of kids who look happy when Mr. Knight gives them back the math test we took yesterday. Even Mr. Knight looks happy, which means there must have been lots of good grades.

I cross my toes. I hope my name will be added to the happy list.

When Mr. Knight gets to my desk, his smile disappears. "Mallory, may I see you before you leave for lunch."

I nod and try to look like it's no big deal. But I know Mr. Knight wanting to see me can only mean one thing. I didn't do well. I pretend like I'm at the wish pond on my street and make a quick wish before I look down at the paper in my hand.

I wish Mr. Knight wants to see me because I did so well he wants to congratulate me personally.

When I finish wishing and look at my test, I know my wish won't be coming true. I made a D on my test! Not an A, a B, or a C. I made a D!

I try to swallow, but I feel like my math book is stuck in my throat. I've never made

such a bad grade. I check the name on
the top of the test to make sure Mr. Knight
didn't give me someone else's test, but it
says *Mallory McDonald* in my handwriting.

I look up and see Arielle
and Danielle mouthing
something to each other
from across the room. I
don't know what they're
saying, but I do know
they're pointing to me when
they say it.

I also know that whatever they're saying
to each other can't be nearly as bad as
what Mr. Knight is going to say to me
before lunch.

Usually, the mornings at school go by
slowly, but this morning speeds by. It
feels like seconds, not hours, from the
time Mr. Knight gives back the math

tests to the time he dismisses everyone for lunch.

All my friends walk out without me. I stay behind to talk to my teacher.

"Mallory," says Mr. Knight. "I'm upset to see how poorly you did on your math test. You've always been a good student, but lately, you've not been paying attention in class, and now, your grades are slipping."

Mr. Knight stops talking and looks at me like it's my turn to say something, but I'm not sure what to say. "I'm sorry," I mumble in a quiet voice.

"Mallory, is there a reason for your change in habits? If something is going on, you should tell me so I can help you."

I look at my teacher. There is something going on. *I have a crush on a boy who likes someone else with long, blonde hair and big, blue eyes, and I can't exactly spend all my time thinking about math when I have to think about how to get the boy to stop liking her and start liking me.*

That's what's going on, but something tells me I can't tell that to Mr. Knight, and even if I could, I don't think it's something he could help me with.

Mr. Knight looks at me like he's waiting for my answer.

I shrug my shoulders like I don't have a good answer.

"Mallory, you need to show your test to your parents tonight and have them sign it." Mr. Knight is quiet for a moment. Then he keeps talking. "I'm going to ask them to come in for a conference. We need to nip this in the bud."

When he says that, Mr. Knight sounds more like a gardener than a teacher. But I know he's not talking about flowers.

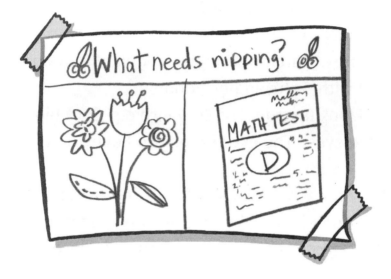

"You may go eat your lunch now," says Mr. Knight.

I walk to the cafeteria, but lunch is the last thing on my mind. I don't know how I can eat when all I can think about is Mr. Knight calling my parents.

When I walk into the cafeteria, I'm so busy thinking about Mr. Knight talking to Mom and Dad that I don't even see two people walking toward me until after it's too late.

"Hey, watch where you're going!" says a girl with a tray in her hand.

I look up from the tray into a pair of big, blue eyes. The eyes belong to Bailey and she's with JT.

"Aren't you Max's little sister?" asks JT.

I don't know why, but all of a sudden, I'm speechless. I nod my head *yes*. I've never been so happy to be Max's sister.

Bailey looks at JT and laughs. "She's the one that dropped her tray last week."

JT nods like it all makes sense to him now, and then he smiles. "Watch where you're going. You don't want to have any more accidents."

Before I can say anything like *I only had the accident because I was trying to get your attention* or *It's clear we belong together*, JT and Bailey walk off.

I can't believe I finally had a chance to talk to JT and all I did was nod. I find my friends and sit down with them.

I open my lunch bag and take out my sandwich, but I can't eat. It's like my brain just shifted gears. One minute, I was thinking about what my parents are going to say when they see my math test. The next minute, all I can think about is what JT just said to me. He doesn't want me to "*have any more accidents.*"

Maybe he doesn't want me to have any more accidents because he doesn't want anything to happen to me.

Maybe he doesn't want me to have any more accidents because he secretly likes me just like I secretly like him.

Maybe he doesn't want me to have any more accidents because when he thinks of the future, he can't bear to think of it without me.

"What did he want?" asks Pamela.

"What did he say?" asks April.

Mary Ann taps my head with a spoon. "Earth to Mallory!" she says.

"Huh? What?" I start to tell them who I just bumped into, but I realize my friends aren't talking about JT. They want to know what happened with Mr. Knight.

I tell them what he said about not paying attention in class and how I did on my math test. I tell them that he's going to call my parents.

When I'm done talking, Pamela frowns. "Mallory, you're a good student. But you're going to have to face the facts. If you want to do well, you have to study more. If you want me to, I can help you make flash cards."

"That's a good idea," says April.

Mary Ann nods like she thinks so too.

I can't help looking around the cafeteria to see if I can find JT.

Mary Ann bops me on the head with her milk carton. "Mallory! Pay attention! Do you want Pamela to help you make flash cards?"

I see JT and Bailey by the juice dispenser. "That would be great," I tell Pamela.

I know I should be facing the facts, especially the ones that have to do with fractions and decimal points. But the truth is, it's hard to face those facts when all I can think about is that the boy I like is off with another girl.

And that's a fact.

CONFERENCE TIME

I hold up two outfits.

Outfit #1: Black leggings with a black sweatshirt.

Outfit #2: Black skirt with a black T-shirt.

Cheeseburger gives me a *you're-going-to-a-parent-conference-not-a-funeral* look. But I can't help that I'm in a dark mood.

I think back to last night. My parents were not happy about my test. They were even more upset when Mr. Knight called. Even though I couldn't hear what my teacher was saying, just hearing what my parents had to say was enough to know that I'm in big trouble.

The good news last night was that my parents said we could wait to have *our* talk until after they have *their* talk with Mr. Knight.

The bad news is that they said they wanted all the facts before deciding what to do with me.

I decide to go with outfit #1.

When I'm dressed, I walk into the kitchen. Mom and Dad are already at the table.

I tell my parents good morning, but I can see by the looks on their faces that they don't think the morning is so good.

Mom puts a plate of eggs and toast in front of me. "Mallory, eat your breakfast. Dad and I are going to drive you and Max to school."

Max walks into the kitchen and takes a piece of toast out of the toaster. Then he looks out the window. "It's not raining. Why are you driving us to school? It's two blocks away." He takes a big bite of toast.

Mom and Dad look at each other.

"We have a meeting," says Mom.

Max swallows his toast. "If you and Dad both have a meeting at school, it can only be about one of two things." He looks at me and grins. "I didn't do anything wrong."

I put a big bite of eggs in my mouth. The last person I want to talk to about why Mom and Dad are coming to school is my brother.

Unfortunately, it is the only thing Max wants to talk about. "So what did you do?" he asks me. "Talk back to the teacher? Disrupt the class? Make a bad grade?"

I put my fork down. Sometimes my brother makes me so mad. "I didn't talk back to the teacher or disrupt the class!" I tell Max.

He makes a face like he just discovered the lost treasure. "So you made a bad grade. Well, if you were spending more time thinking about school and less time thinking about JT that wouldn't have happened."

Mom and Dad look at each other.

"Max, this is none of your business," says Mom.

Dad looks at me. "What is JT?"

Max laughs. "JT is a *who* not a *what*. He's in my class, and Mallory has a crush on him. If you ask me, Mallory should be spending less time thinking about someone she doesn't even know and more time thinking about her schoolwork. "

Dad looks at Mom like he doesn't like the sound of this.

"Mallory, you like a boy?" he asks.

I nod that I do.

Dad keeps asking questions. "Do you know this boy?"

"I can answer that one," says Max. "No."

Dad looks confused. "You like a boy, but you don't know this boy?"

This was not how I pictured my *first love* talk with my parents to happen. "I can explain it," I say to Dad.

Dad gives me a *you'll-have-plenty-of-time-to-explain-later* look. "We have to go or we'll be late."

When we get to school, the hallways are still empty. It feels weird to be at school so early when no one is here yet, but it feels even weirder to be here with my parents.

When we get to my classroom, Mr. Knight is already there. "Mallory, why don't you wait in the hallway. I'd like a few minutes alone with your parents."

I swallow and nod like that's fine, but it doesn't feel fine.

When the door closes behind Mom and Dad, I press my ear against the door, but I can't hear a word.

I thought I was going to be part of the conference too.

I try not to think about what Mr. Knight is saying.

Mallory is failing math.
Mallory doesn't pay attention.
Mallory doesn't belong in the classroom.
Mallory should be locked in her room.
Forever.

I try not to think about what my parents
are saying.

*Mallory is wasting
her time thinking about
a boy.*

*A boy she doesn't
even know.*

*He might be
dangerous.*

*He should be sent to
a foreign country.*

Forever.

I look in the little
window on the door
of our classroom.

Mr. Knight doesn't look too happy and neither do my parents.

Thinking about what they're saying about me and the boy I like is bad enough, but imagining what they're going to do to us is even worse.

I press my ear against the door again. I really wish I could hear what was going on.

Whoever invented doors for school classrooms should get a medal. This thing is soundproof.

Whoever invented parent-teacher conferences should be sent to a foreign country.

Forever.

A DATE

This weekend, I have a date.
With my math book.
Mom and Dad said that I need to spend
more time studying. They said I need
to stop thinking about boys, especially
ones that I don't know, and start thinking
about school. They said I am grounded
and not allowed to leave my room except
for meals.

They said a lot of other things too including no friends, no phone, and no computer.

I plop down on my bed with Cheeseburger and my math book. "It's just you and me and this book," I say to my cat.

But the minute I say that, Champ walks into my room and jumps onto my bed.

Ugh! Champ smells terrible. I try to push him off the bed, but he doesn't budge.

"I'm the one who is grounded, not you," I say to Champ. "You're free to go." I give him a little push, but he still doesn't budge.

I hold my nose and push a little harder. "Why don't you go in Max's room and wait for him until he gets back from baseball, and maybe he'll give you a bath."

But all Champ does is scoot closer to me and close his eyes.

I don't know how Champ can sleep with
that smell. I know I couldn't sleep with that
smell. And I definitely can't do math.

"C'mon," I say to Champ. "If Max won't
give you a bath, I will."

I pull Champ by the collar until he
follows me into the bathroom. I close the
door and turn on the water. I've never
actually given Champ a bath so I'm not
really sure where to start.

But I finish before I ever get started.

Mom opens the door to the bathroom. "Mallory Louise McDonald, you are supposed to be studying, not giving Champ a bath." She turns the water off.

I try to explain how hard it is to study with a smelly dog in my room, but Mom says it's time to stop focusing on the dog and start focusing on math.

She points me toward my desk.

I take a deep breath and sit down. I know it won't do any good to argue with Mom. I start with the page of extra practice problems that Mr. Knight gave me.

I do practice problem #1.

Practice problem #2.

Practice problem #3.

Practice problem #4.

And practice problem #5.

I start on practice problem #6, but as soon as I do, I hear a noise.

Someone is knocking on my window.

There is only one person who ever knocks on my window. I run to the window and pull my curtain aside. It's just who I thought it was. Mary Ann!

Even though Mom and Dad said *no friends*, they did not say *no best friends*.

I open my window and put my finger to my lips. "We have to be quiet." I remind her that I'm grounded.

Mary Ann nods like she knows and doesn't need to be reminded. "I wouldn't even be here except that I have something V.I.T.T.Y."

I make a face like I'm not sure what she meant.

"I have something *very important to tell you*," she whispers.

I love important things. "What is it?" I whisper back.

Mary Ann clears her throat like she is about to make an important announcement.

For someone who is supposed to be quiet, she is not doing a very good job. I look around to make sure I don't hear any footsteps in the hallway.

"So what is the important thing?" I whisper.

Mary Ann looks around like now she wants to be sure that no one is listening to her, and then she starts talking.

"I heard Winnie talking on the phone this morning. She was talking to Bailey, who is going to the movies this afternoon."

Mary Ann pauses like she's waiting for me to say something and I do. "Why should I care that Bailey is going to the movies this afternoon?" I ask Mary Ann.

Mary Ann keeps talking. "I heard Winnie telling her that she should wear her denim miniskirt with the pink and black striped top."

I roll my eyes. "Why should I care what Bailey is wearing to the movies?" I ask Mary Ann.

Mary Ann shakes her head like I don't get it, and then she keeps talking. "I heard Winnie tell Bailey that she should straighten her hair and part it in the middle."

Now I'm really confused and I'm running out of patience. I really don't want Mom to come in my room and see me talking to Mary Ann. "Why in the world should I care where Bailey is going and what she is wearing and how she is styling her hair?"

Mary Ann looks at me like I'm from another planet. "Mallory, the reason I'm telling you all this is not because you need to know where Bailey is going or what she's wearing or how she's styling her hair. I'm telling you all this because you should know *who* she's going with."

But before Mary Ann even gets to the *who* part, I know the answer. "Is she going with JT?" I ask.

Mary Ann nods. Then she looks like she's sorry she had to be the one to tell me.

I hear footsteps coming toward my door. "You should go," I whisper.

Mary Ann waves good-bye, and I close my curtain.

As soon as I sit back down at my desk, my door opens.

"Everything OK in here?" Mom asks.

I put my pencil on practice problem #6. "It definitely is," I tell Mom.

But the truth is, it definitely, definitely is not.

A LOVE STORY

Max opens my door and walks into my room. His baseball cleats leave a trail of dirt on my floor. "Still grounded, huh?"

I give Max a dirty look. I know he's not expecting an answer. He knows I'm in my room for a while.

"Get out!" I tell him. "I'm trying to do my math."

"Don't let me stop you," says Max. "C'mon, Champ!" His dog follows him out of my room.

When they are gone, I try to do my math. I really, really try.

I am still on practice problem #6. I look at the clock. I have been on practice problem #6 for twenty minutes, and I still have twenty-four more to go before I'm done.

I try doing practice problems sitting at my desk. I try doing practice problems lying on my bed. I try doing practice problems spread out on my floor.

But no matter where I do practice problems or how I do them, I can't get my brain to think about practice problems when it is busy thinking about JT and Bailey at the movies.

I put away my math and get out a pen and a sheet of paper.

I'm not in the mood to do math, but I am in the mood to do some writing.

A LOVE STORY

By Mallory McDonald

(Note to reader: This is a love story with a happy ending. Love stories are supposed to have happy endings. But some weird things happen in the middle of this story. Some of the things have to do with animals. So if you are an animal lover, don't get upset. Keep reading! The ending is a HUGE, HAPPY surprise. You will love it. I promise. OK. Now you can start reading.)

Once upon a time, there was a couple named Bailey + JT. (Don't those names sound horrible together?)

Everyone (except for one girl with red hair and freckles who lives at 17 Wish Pond Road, but I don't want to name names) said they made a cute couple.

Maybe they did at first, but not for long.

Here's why:

One Saturday, Bailey and JT went to the movies together. That is where all of their problems started.

Bailey, who was pretty and sweet and funny and popular (according to some people, but not the girl with red hair and freckles), ate some popcorn that must have been spoiled because when she ate it, she turned into the ugliest, bumpiest, slimiest, smelliest toad ever.

I know that sounds like something that would happen in

a fairy tale, but it happened at the Fern Falls Cineplex.

When it did, JT completely freaked out. He started jumping up and down in his seat and screamed, "I don't want a toad for a girlfriend!"

Other people in the theater got really annoyed because they couldn't see or hear the movie with JT jumping around and making so much noise.

So JT said to Bailey, "Get lost." And Bailey had no choice but to hop away home.

OK. That was the upsetting part having to do with animals. Here's where the "love" part begins.

JT looked down in his hand and realized he still had Bailey's movie ticket. He wanted someone to share the movie with. His mind quickly went to the girl in

the cafeteria with the rain boots and the sunglasses. He knew that was the girl for him.

But he didn't know her phone number. He decided to just guess. He started punching numbers into his cell phone, and he got it right the first time.

Rain boots, sunglasses girl (who happens to be the same redhead with freckles who lives at 17 Wish Pond Road that I mentioned earlier in the story) answered the phone. When JT invited her to join him at the movies, she said she would love to.

Her parents (who had grounded her) ungrounded her and said she could go. Her

dad even offered to do her math for her while her mom drove her to the theater.

When she arrived, JT was waiting outside for her. They went into the theater where they watched the movie and shared a bucket of unspoiled popcorn. They laughed and had an AMAZING time together. JT must have told the girl like a thousand times what an AMAZING time he had.

OK. Warning for animal lovers: The next part of the story is a tiny bit upsetting, but it is over quickly. Then it gets happy again.

That night, there was a report on the news that the ugliest, bumpiest, slimiest, smelliest toad ever seen in Fern Falls hopped all the way to Australia and then was kidnapped by a band of kangaroos and would never be seen again.

JT saw the news report, but he didn't care.

He said ugly, bumpy, slimy, smelly toads made him hyper and jumpy and that he had already found the girl of his dreams right here in Fern Falls.

(In case you were doing something else like painting your nails or watching

TV while you read this, the girl he was talking about was the one with red hair and freckles that lives at 17 Wish Pond Road.)

THE END (Isn't it a happy one!?!)

Actually, it gets a little happier. Keep reading...

The girl (with red hair and freckles) found out that JT's grade in math had dropped recently for the same reason hers had dropped.

He had been spending too much time thinking about her and not doing his practice problems! What a coincidence!!!

So the girl and JT decided to study together. And when they did, both of their grades went from Ds (that's what JT had too) to A+s and both of their parents were really, really, really happy about that. Also, their teachers gave them both awards for having the highest math grades in their classes.

THE REAL END

(I told you it was happy!)

Fern Falls Cutest Couple and Math Super Students!

ON THE PHONE

"Mallory, telephone!" I can hear Max shouting for me from the kitchen.

I run down the hall to get it.

"Mallory, keep it short," says Mom when I come into the kitchen. "You have homework to do, and you know how your father and I feel about you using the phone."

I know exactly how they feel. Mom says I spent a lot of time on the phone this week. Dad says I spent too much time on the phone this week. Max said I should be banned from using it ever again.

I was on the phone a lot this week. I talked to Mary Ann (17 times), Joey

(8 times, but 7 of those times were when he answered the phone when I was trying to talk to Mary Ann), Pamela (4 times), Grandma (1 time), and JT (0 times, but I thought about calling him 47 times).

Even though I talked to so many people so many times, there was only one thing I talked about (except for the four times I talked to Pamela about flash cards).

SUNDAY: Phone call with Mary Ann

ME: Hey, Hey, Hey.

MARY ANN: Hey, Hey, Hey.

ME: So did Winnie say anything else about Bailey and JT going to the movies yesterday?

MARY ANN: Just that they are going again next Saturday.

WHAT I SAID: Oh. *(What I didn't say: Do you think there is any chance the movie theater will go out of business before next Saturday?)*

MARY ANN: Mallory, you don't even know JT. Why do you care if he and Bailey go to the movies?

ME: I might not know him, but I know I like him.

MARY ANN: I'm only 10, but it seems to me you should get to know people before you decide if you like them.

WHAT I SAID: You're probably right. *(What I didn't say: Except for in this case. I don't need to get to know JT to know that I like him. I knew I liked him the first time I looked at him. All any girl would have to do to know she likes him is to look at him. Plus, he's really popular. If everybody else likes JT, why shouldn't I?)*

MONDAY: Phone call with Joey *(Actually, it was supposed to be a phone call with Mary Ann, but when I called, Joey answered the phone.)*

JOEY: Let me guess. It's Mallory calling for Mary Ann so she can talk for the three thousandth time today about a boy she thinks she likes but doesn't even know?

ME: If you knew I wanted to talk to Mary Ann, why did you pick up the phone?

JOEY: What if there's an emergency and someone at one of our houses actually needs to use the phone?

ME: This is an emergency.

JOEY: Define *emergency.*

ME: Today at lunch I saw Bailey and JT sharing a cookie.

JOEY: You need to look up the definition of emergency in the dictionary.

WHAT I SAID: Ha, ha, ha. *(What I didn't say: Not funny at all!)*

TUESDAY: Phone call with Pamela

PAMELA: Hey, Mallory. Have you started using the flash cards yet?

WHAT I SAID: They're great. *(What I didn't say: I'm sure they're great, but I don't actually know because I haven't actually used them.)*

PAMELA: I'm glad I could help. I think flash cards are the best way to study.

ME: *(looking at the clock because I have other phone calls not about flash cards to make)* Thanks again for helping me.

PAMELA: If you want more help, you can

come over on Saturday, and I'll review them with you.

WHAT I SAID: That sounds great. *(What I didn't say: If JT decides to dump Bailey this week, I want to be available to go to the movies with him on Saturday.)*

WEDNESDAY: Phone call with Mary Ann (and unfortunately, Joey)

MARY ANN: Hey. Hey. Hey. What's up?

ME: So did Winnie say anything else about Bailey and JT? Like maybe they broke up? Or maybe he choked on the cookie she gave him and he wants a new girlfriend?

MARY ANN: *(about to talk but gets interrupted before she starts)*

JOEY: Hi, Mallory. It's Joey.

ME: Haven't you heard of private conversations? I think there's a law about it. You can't open other people's mail, and you can't listen in on their phone conversations.

JOEY TO ME: *(ignoring everything I just said)* This whole JT thing has to stop. It's completely ridiculous and it's boring too. There are more important things in the world.

ME TO JOEY: Name one.

JOEY TO ME: Skateboarding.

(What I didn't say: How can you think skateboarding is more important than JT?)

JOEY TO MARY ANN: Come in the kitchen. It's time for dinner.

MARY ANN TO JOEY: I'll be right there.

MARY ANN TO ME: I'll call you after dinner.

THURSDAY: Phone call with Grandma

GRANDMA: Honey bee, how are you?

ME: I'm fine, Grandma. How are you?

GRANDMA: Well, I have to admit, I'm a little curious.

ME: *(not liking the way this sounds)* About what?

GRANDMA: Your mom told me that you have a little crush. I just had to hear it from my Honey Bee myself. *(a muffled sound like Grandma is getting all choked up)* You're getting so big and so grown-up.

ME: I haven't gotten any bigger since you saw me over the holidays.

GRANDMA: *(laughing)* That wasn't exactly what I meant.

FRIDAY: Phone call with JT *(actually, phone call I imagined having with JT)*

JT: Hey, Mallory. What's up?

ME: *(In a very cool, grown-up voice)* Not much. I'm just hanging out.

JT: Cool. So listen, I'm calling because I'm going to go see a movie tomorrow and I wanted to see if you wanted to come see it with me.

ME: I thought you were going with Bailey to the movies.

JT: Bailey? Who's Bailey?

ME: I'd love to go to the movies with you.

JT: Good, because if you said you didn't want to go, I'd probably start crying or something like that. I know everyone thinks I like Bailey. But I don't. You are the girl for me. Let me say it again (in a really loud voice): YOU ARE THE GIRL FOR ME!!!

"Max, give it to me!" I say.

I try to take the receiver from Max. He holds it away from me like he's not going to give it up so easily. "Guess who it's not?" he says.

I roll my eyes and try to ignore my brother. He finally gives me the phone and I say hello to my best friend.

For the eighteenth time this week.

THE PERFECT PLAN

It's Saturday morning at eight thirty and I have a plan.

Actually, it's Saturday morning at eight thirty and I have a GREAT plan.

It's a plan to get JT's attention. I know I've had other plans to get JT's attention that haven't worked, but I have a new plan.

If I had to give my new plan a name, I'd call it *The Perfect Plan*.

If you're wondering how I could come up with a perfect plan so early on a Saturday morning, you can stop wondering. I'll tell you. I woke up, and it was like the plan popped into my head right when I opened my eyes.

That's how I know it's a perfect plan. . . . I didn't even have to think about it.

I cross my toes and pretend like I'm at the wish pond on my street.

All I have to do is to put *The Perfect Plan* into place.

Step 1.

I put on my blue jeans, purple and pink polka-dotted shirt, sparkly purple sneakers, and matching headband. I look in the mirror and smile. The outfit is just right for the occasion.

Step 2.

I take a piece of paper out of my desk, write the address that I need on it, carefully fold it into a little square, and slip it into my back pocket.

Step 3.

I check the movie times in the paper. The Saturday afternoon movies don't start until one thirty. I check my watch. I have plenty of time.

Step 4.

I go over my plan with my cat. "Cheeseburger, pay attention!" I say.

I point to the easel in my bedroom and explain how the plan is going to work.

"When Mom leaves to take Max to baseball and to go to the grocery store and when Dad goes outside to mow the yard and trim the hedges, I'm going to bake the cookies. When the cookies are baked, I'll quickly take them to JT. He'll realize that Bailey never baked delicious cookies for him.

We'll talk and laugh and eat cookies, and he'll tell me he's liked the wrong girl all along, but he's not going to do that anymore. He'll tell me that from now on when he goes to the movies, he's going with me. Then I'll come home before anyone even knows I'm gone."

When I'm done talking, Cheeseburger purrs.

I'm glad my cat likes my plan as much as I do.

When I go into the kitchen, Max is packing his baseball bag and Mom and Dad are finishing their coffee. Mom puts a plate of waffles in front of me.

"Mallory, I'm dropping Max off at baseball, going to the store, and I'll be home after he's done with practice," says Mom. "While I'm gone, I want you to do your math homework. You want to be ready for your test on Monday."

I nod, like that's exactly what I want. And I do want that. But there are some other things I want too.

Dad winks at me. "Sweet Potato, I'll be outside making the McDonalds' front yard look beautiful. If you need any help with your math, feel free to interrupt my lawn duties."

I nod at Dad. I know I'm supposed to be doing math this morning, but part of *The Perfect Plan* is that I will be doing math this afternoon.

I watch while Mom puts the breakfast dishes in the dishwasher and

Max packs a water bottle in his baseball bag and laces his cleats. My stomach does a little flip-flop.

Step 5.

I wait for everyone in my family to go do their thing.

Step 6.

When they're gone, I do mine.

LOST AND FOUND

I didn't realize how hard it is to bake.

I look at the tray of cookies I just took out of the oven. The bad news is they don't look as good as the ones I made with Mom. In fact, they don't look anything like the ones I made with Mom. The good news is you can still tell they're cookies. Sort of.

Some of the cookies stick to the cookie sheet when I try taking them off. A few of them break into pieces when I put them on the plate. I mash the broken ones back together with my fingers and scrape the stuck ones off the tray.

My plate of cookies doesn't look at all like the one I pictured in my head or on my easel, but it will have to do. I wrap foil around the top of the plate and look around the kitchen. When I do, I groan. There are only two words to describe it. HUGE MESS!

Actually, there are four words. HUGE, HUGE, HUGE MESS!!!

I look at the clock. Mom will be home soon, and Dad will be done mowing the lawn. The cookies took a lot longer to make than I thought they would. I take a deep breath. *The Perfect Plan* isn't going quite as perfectly as I had planned.

Part of me feels like I should stop and
not follow my plan. Part of me feels like I
should clean up before I go. And another
part of me knows I need to hurry or I won't
have time to take the cookies to JT and get
back in time.

I look out the kitchen window. Dad is
still mowing. I pick up the cookies and

decide to go. I'll just have to hurry so I'll have time to clean up when I get back.

As I start to walk out the back door, Cheeseburger wedges herself between the door and me like she doesn't want me to go.

"Are you a cat or a stop sign?" I bend down and pet Cheeseburger, and she gives me a look. I can't help wondering if it is a *taking-cookies-to-a-boy-I-don't-know-is-a-bad-idea* look.

Eenie Meenie Miney Mo.
Should I stay, clean, or go?

I push the door open and push the *should-I-stay* thoughts out of my head. "I'll be back soon," I tell my cat. I slip out the back door and start down Wish Pond Road.

When I get to the end of my street, I take the square of paper that I wrote JT's address on out of my back pocket. So far so good.

1245 Lilly Lane.

I'm pretty sure Lilly Lane is behind the Fern Falls Village Shopping Center. I turn right and walk until I get to the shopping center. When we drive from our house to the shopping center, it seems like it doesn't take any time at all, but it takes longer than I thought it would to walk.

I stop at the bus stop in front of the shopping center for a minute to rest.

I'm hot and thirsty. I look down at the piece of paper in my hand. I know I need to keep going. When I get to JT's house, I will ask him for something to drink.

I look around before I start walking and try to picture Lilly Lane. I know I've passed it lots of times, and I know it's near the shopping center. I thought I would know which way to go when I got here, but now I'm a little confused.

Eenie Meenie Miney Mo.
Help me decide which way to go.

I turn right and keep walking. Lilly Lane can't be too far.

I pass Stanley Street and Cecilia Circle and Amanda Avenue.

I keep walking. I pass lots of streets named after lots of people, but none of them are named after Lilly.

I stop and sit down under a tree to rest. Maybe I should have turned left instead of turning right. Maybe I should eat a cookie.

I'm thirsty and I'm hungry too. I take a cookie from the plate and take a bite. It doesn't taste like a cookie. It tastes like dried-up play dough, and tasting it makes me even thirstier than I was before.

I get up. I have to keep walking.

I turn left and pass back by all the streets I passed before. When I get back to the bus stop in front of the shopping center, I keep walking. Lilly Lane has to be somewhere close by.

I pass Randolph Road and Billy Boulevard and lots and lots of other roads and streets and circles and boulevards and lanes, but not one with a sign on it that says Lilly.

I keep walking. I turn left and I turn right. I walk until I feel like I can't walk anymore and still no sign of Lilly Lane.

I sit down on the sidewalk. All of a sudden, I feel hot and thirsty and hungry and pretty sure that Lilly Lane isn't where I thought it was.

I look around. This neighborhood doesn't look familiar to me at all.

My throat feels tight, but not because it's thirsty.

I'm not sure how to get to JT's house, and now I'm not even sure how to get back to my own house. All of a sudden, my plan doesn't seem so perfect. In fact, it seems like it is only getting me one place . . . and

that one place is lost.

I am lost.

I, Mallory McDonald, am officially LOST.

Just thinking about it makes me cry. I never should have left home.

I should have stayed to clean up and play with Cheeseburger. I think about my house and my parents and even my brother. The more I think about everything at home, the harder I cry.

I wipe my nose on my sleeve.

The sidewalk I'm sitting on is starting to feel hot, so I move to a patch of grass in someone's front yard. I look around, there's a little fountain in their yard and some tomato plants. I wonder if I will have to spend the rest of my life sleeping on this little patch of grass, bathing in the fountain, and eating tomatoes.

Thinking about that makes me cry harder and harder.

I lie down on the grass and use the plate of cookies I made for JT as a pillow.

I think about my family again. I wonder if they will know I am gone and if they will come looking for me.

I feel like I lie there for a long, long time. I close my eyes. When I feel someone shaking my shoulder, I open them. It's a lady. A strange lady.

I swallow and pretend like I'm at the wish pond on my street and make a wish.

I wish she will be a nice lady who is going to help me.

"I'm Mrs. Walker," she says in a kind voice. "I noticed you lying down in my front yard. Are you OK?"

I try to wipe away my tears on my shirt. I tell Mrs. Walker what happened. She listens and asks for my phone number. Mrs. Walker takes her cell phone out of her pocket and dials my number. I can hear Mom's voice on the other end of the phone.

"Your parents are on their way," she says.

I smile. "Thank you."

Mrs. Walker smiles back. "We'll just wait right here until they arrive."

We don't have to wait for long. When I see Mom's minivan coming down the street, I take a big, deep breath. I have never been so happy to see her car.

Mom and Dad pull up in front of Mrs. Walker's house, and when they do, I run to the van. Mom and Dad get out, and they both give me a big hug.

I'm found! I can't believe I've been found. I don't know why, but being found makes me cry even harder than being lost. "I'm so happy to see you," I tell my parents.

I wait for them to tell me they are happy to see me too, but that's not what they say.

"Mallory Louise McDonald, get in the car," says Dad in his serious voice.

When Dad uses that voice, I know I should just do what he says and not say anything. I get in the car and close the door. I watch while Mom and Dad talk to Mrs. Walker.

When Mom and Dad get in the car, they don't say a word to each other or to me.

When we pull into our driveway, Dad finally speaks.

"Mallory, go to your room. You need to spend some time thinking about everything you've done. Mom and I will talk to you when we're ready."

When we walk into the house, Max shakes his head like he wouldn't want to be me. "Someone is in BIG trouble," he says under his breath.

For once, I agree with Max. Someone is in BIG trouble, and that someone is me.

Cheeseburger follows me to my room. When we get inside, I close the door and collapse on my bed. I've never seen Dad look so mad, and Mom didn't look any happier. I can feel the tears starting again. Cheeseburger hops onto my bed next to me.

I rub the fur on her back and she sighs. I know cats can't talk, but if mine could, I think she'd tell me that I'm going to be in a whole lot of trouble.

And I think my cat is right.

LETTER IN A BOTTLE

I wipe away my tears. Then I look at my four walls.

Mom and Dad said they would be in to talk to me when they are ready, but they aren't here yet. "What if they're never coming?" I ask my cat.

I pick up Cheeseburger and squeeze her tight. "What if Mom and Dad are so mad at me, they're planning to leave me in my room forever?" I wish I had a rewind button and I could push it and redo this day. Nothing about it has been good.

I count to ten slowly. Then I wait and count again. Still no sign of Mom and Dad.

I can feel it, and I think Cheeseburger can too. No one is coming for us.

"Don't worry," I say to my cat. "I will get us out of here."

I pat Cheeseburger, sit down at my desk, and take out a sheet of paper. Then I blow my nose and start on T.M.I.L.O.M.L. (Short for *The Most Important Letter of My Life.*)

Dear To-Whom-It-May-Concern,

I am a young girl who has been sent to my room. I don't want to get into the specifics of what I did. I just want to say that my parents have sent me to my room and I don't think they are planning to let me out for a long time.

It could be for years.

So if you find this letter, please come rescue me. My name is Mallory McDonald. I live at 17 Wish Pond Road.

I want to make sure nothing gets in the way of my rescue, so you should probably rescue me through my window.

It is the second window downstairs on the left side of the house.

When you come, please bring some things that I will need.

The most important thing to bring are doughnuts. Some apple juice would be nice too.

Since I don't know how long I'm in here for, I can't be sure my parents will have given me food (or at least food that I like) and I will probably be starving.

Also, can you please bring me something to wear?

If I am going to be rescued, I want to look cute. If you are not sure what to bring, watch a few episodes of *Fashion Fran*. If you are still not sure or if you're not a "fashion" person and need some help picking something that you think will look *rescue chic*, go next door and ask my best, best, best friend, Mary Ann, for help.

One more thing. Please bring food for my cat, Cheeseburger, and purple polish for my toes (sorry, I know that is two things).

Here is something you should think about: if you rescue me, you will probably be a local hero and maybe even get in the newspaper or on TV, so you should wear something cute too.

If you want, we can match. I bet there has never been a rescue when the rescuer and the recue-ee match. I think that will be very cute.

Oh yeah, also, do you think we should plan to make rescue speeches? Since I am stuck in my room, I will have a lot of time to work on mine, but you should work on yours.

Thanks so, so, so much. See you soon (I hope).

Sincerely,
Mallory McDonald

When I'm done writing, I roll up my letter and put it in an empty Coke bottle that I had used as a bracelet holder. If I lived near the ocean, I would throw my letter in a bottle so someone could find it and rescue me.

I look out my window. If I ever get out of my room, the wish pond is going to have to do.

DOUBLE
TROUBLE

Knock. Knock. Knock.

I jump when I hear someone knocking
at my door. I look down at the bottle in
my hand. Something tells me it's not my
rescuer.

When I open the door, Mom and Dad are
on the other side. They both have serious
looks on their faces.

"Mallory, we need to talk," Dad says.

"You're in a lot of trouble, young lady."

Mom has an *I-agree-with-everything-your-father-has-to-say* look on her face.

I don't like when I'm in trouble with one parent. But it's even worse when both of them are mad. I know Dad said I'm in trouble, but I feel like I'm in double trouble.

Dad crosses his arms across his chest and starts talking.

"Mallory, Mom and I are very upset with you. What you did this morning was wrong in so many ways. You used the oven without permission. You could have burned yourself. You left a big mess in the kitchen. And the worst part was that you left home without permission."

Dad stops and looks at me like he wants to make sure I am paying attention to every word he says. "You wandered around Fern Falls, alone, not even knowing where you were going. All kinds of bad things could have happened to you. Do you understand that what you did was foolish and unsafe?"

Dad looks at me like he's waiting for me to tell him that I do understand or explain my behavior, but before I have a chance to say anything, Dad keeps talking.

"Mallory, Mom and I were very worried about you and very upset that you didn't use better judgment. What do you have to say for yourself?"

I look at Dad. I can tell by the wrinkles on his forehead that he is really upset.

I look down at the bottle with the letter in it that is still in my hand.

I think the only person that can rescue me now is myself. I know what I did was wrong, and I know that I have a lot of explaining to do.

Dad clears his throat like he's waiting for me to answer, but he doesn't want to wait any longer. "Dad, I'm really sorry about what I did."

Dad looks at me like he wants an explanation, not an apology.

I try to talk, but I know if I do, I will start crying.

I think back to this morning when my plan popped into my head. I really wish I hadn't decided to take cookies to JT. I try to blink back the tears that are forming in the corners of my eyes. I know it was a bad decision.

Dad looks at Mom like it's her turn to talk.

"Mallory, your father and I are having a hard time understanding why you did what you did this morning. We want to know why you baked cookies and where you were going."

A tear falls from my eye to the bottle in my hand. Even though I know Mom and Dad aren't going to understand when I tell them that I baked cookies for JT and was going to take them to him, I know I have to tell them.

When I finish explaining, Mom and Dad look at each other. Then Dad looks at me.

"Mallory, aside from using the oven unsupervised and leaving home without permission, you were taking cookies to a boy that you hardly know. Do you think that is an appropriate way to get to know someone?"

"Taking cookies to JT seemed like a good idea this morning." I try to wipe away my tears. "But I know it wasn't."

Another tear falls, then another, and another.

Dad sits down beside me and hands me a tissue.

"Mom, Dad, I'm really sorry about everything I did. I know I shouldn't have used the oven without permission. I know it wasn't a good idea to leave home without telling you where I was going. And I know I shouldn't have tried to take cookies to JT. I was just trying to do something to get him to like me."

Dad puts his arm around me. "Mallory, can you please tell me why it was so important to you to get JT to like you.

You don't really know him, so how do you even know you like him?"

I look down at the tissue in my hand. I have to think about my answer.

"He's really cute," I say.

Dad doesn't respond.

"And he's popular."

Dad just looks at me like it's still my turn to talk.

I know what I'm saying doesn't make a lot of sense to my parents. The truth is, it doesn't even make much sense to me. "I guess those aren't reasons to like someone, are they?"

Dad nods like I'm starting to get it, and I do. I keep talking. "I think I liked the idea of liking a boy more than I really liked the boy."

Dad squeezes my shoulders. "Sweet Potato, you are ten. For now, the important things for you to be thinking about are your family, your friends, and your schoolwork. You have lots of time in the future to be thinking about boys. And believe me, when the time is right, there will be plenty of boys who will be thinking about you."

I dab my eyes with the tissue. "How do you know?" I ask Dad.

Mom and Dad both laugh. "I just do," says Dad.

I don't know why, but hearing my parents laugh, makes me laugh too. I don't know how I can be crying one minute and laughing the next, but all of a sudden, I can't stop laughing.

Mom and Dad laugh with me, and then they both stop and look serious again.

"Mallory Louise McDonald," they say my name together like they both remembered at exactly the same time why they came in my room to talk to me. "You are still in a lot of trouble."

MORE ADDITION

I think back to last night. All I did was math. That is, when I wasn't doing chores.

The bad news is that I will be doing lots of math and lots of chores for a long, long time. The good news is that since I am grounded for a long, long time, I will have plenty of time to do both.

Last night after I washed the dinner dishes, I mopped the kitchen floor, and then I swept the garage. Max said he has never seen a kid do more chores than I did. I could tell even he felt bad for me because he helped me take out the trash.

When I was done washing, mopping, and sweeping, I did math problems. I did them until my fingers ached, my brain was exhausted, and my eyes were practically crossed.

I did so many math problems that the world's smartest mathematician would have a hard time counting all the math problems that I did.

I take a sip of orange juice. "I sure hope all my hard work pays off," I say to Dad.

Dad smiles like he's confident that it will and puts another pancake on my plate. "Hard work and a good breakfast is a surefire way to do well on your math test."

I stuff my mouth with pancakes. I hope Dad is right.

On the way to school, Mary Ann, Joey, and I talk about the math test. I tell them how much I studied.

"You're prepared," says Joey. "I'm sure you'll do well."

"You wore your lucky socks," says Mary Ann pointing down to the bottom part of my legs. "With those on, you're going to ace the test!"

As we walk in the door of Room 404, Pamela comes over to me. She called last night while I was studying and I couldn't even stop to talk.

"Did you use the flash cards?" she asks. I nod that I did.

Pamela smiles like she likes my answer. "Then I'm sure you'll do great."

Pamela is right about most things. I hope she's right about this.

"Class, please get out your science books," says Mr. Knight.

I sit quietly through science and social studies. It's hard to focus on other subjects. Right now, I have a one-track mind, and it's on a math track.

When Mr. Knight finally passes out the math test, I take a deep breath and close my eyes. I pretend like I'm at the wish pond on my street and make a wish.

I wish I will do well on this test.

I pick up my pencil to get started. I try not to think about the butterflies that feel like they've decided to have a family reunion in my stomach. I pretend like I'm at my desk in my room and I'm doing practice problems.

I work my way through page 1. Page 2. And page 3.

I picture the answers on the backs of the flash cards that Pamela made for me.

I force my brain to focus on math and nothing else.

When I'm done with the test, I go back and check my work the way Mr. Knight taught us to do.

"Time to turn in your tests," says Mr. Knight just as I finish checking.

He walks around the classroom and collects the papers.

At lunch, Mary Ann talks about a new episode of *Fashion Fran*.

Pamela talks about her upcoming violin concert.

Arielle and Danielle can't stop talking about a movie they went to.

"Mallory, you're awfully quiet," says April.

I take a bite of my peanut butter and marshmallow sandwich. "I can't stop thinking about the math test. I really hope I did well."

"You'll find out this afternoon," says Pamela. "Mr. Knight says he's grading the tests during lunch and will give them back at the end of the day."

I get the *butterflies-in-my-tummy* feeling again.

Even though all I wanted was to know how I did, now I'm not so sure I do.

After lunch, we do spelling and grammar, and then we see a film about mountain lions. I look at the clock. The bell rings in five minutes.

"Class, I have your math tests graded." Mr. Knight walks around the circle of desks and passes out papers.

Everyone, except for one person, gets their test back, and that one person is me.

When the bell rings, Mr. Knight dismisses everyone. But he stops me. "Mallory, may I see you, please."

Mr. Knight is holding a piece of paper in his hand.

It's the math test I took this morning.

Not again!

"Mallory, we need to talk." His voice sounds serious.

Not a good sign if you ask me.

I try to think fast. I really don't want to hear that I got another bad grade and he needs to see my parents. "Maybe you got my test confused with someone else's," I say.

Mr. Knight looks down at the piece of paper in his hand. "I hope not," he says. Then he smiles and turns the paper around so I can see what he sees. "Because if I did, the other person would be getting an A+ on the test."

I look at the paper Mr. Knight is holding out in front of me. Then I rub my eyes to make sure I'm seeing what I think I see. An A+! I look to make sure it is my paper, and I see my name written in the top right corner in my handwriting.

Wow! No. Scratch that. Wow! Wow! Wow! I want to jump up and down and hug Mr. Knight, but I know that is not a good idea.

"I can't believe I made an A+!" I tell my teacher.

Mr. Knight smiles like he likes seeing the good grade as much as I do. "I saw your mother in the teachers' lounge this morning. She told me how hard you studied."

I nod. Even though my fingers and my brain and my eyes ached when I went to bed last night, now I'm really glad I put in the extra effort.

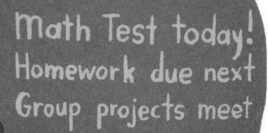

"Mallory, I hope you won't let anything ever get in the way of your schoolwork again," says my teacher.

I hold up two fingers like I'm making a Girl Scout pledge. "I promise that I won't."

Mr. Knight smiles like he approves of my answer. "Keep up the good work," he says. "I'm sure your parents will be proud of you and happy to sign this test."

I think Mr. Knight is right. I can hardly wait to get home to show them. "Can I go now?" I ask Mr. Knight.

Mr. Knight laughs and tells me to hurry home. I run all the way to Wish Pond Road.

When I get inside, Mom is in the kitchen.

"MOM!" I scream her name. Then I hold up my math test so she can see what I made.

Mom gives me a big hug. "Sweet Potato, I am so proud of you, and I know Dad will be too. Why don't you give him a call at work, and you can tell him."

I pick up the phone and dial Dad's number. While I tell him my good news, I watch Mom take ingredients out of the freezer and pantry. Coffee ice cream. Chocolate fudge. A graham cracker pie crust.

"Mom, what are you making?" I ask.

Mom smiles. "Your favorite dinner. Spaghetti and meatballs," she says.

I look at the ingredients on the counter. "I'm not much of a cook," I say to Mom. "But I know there isn't ice cream or fudge in meatballs."

Mom laughs. "I'm also making a special dessert for my special math student."

"What are you making?" I ask.

"A+ Ice Cream Pie." Mom shows me the recipe card, and we both laugh at the name.

A+ Ice Cream Pie

1 11 ounce jar of fudge sauce
1 9-inch graham cracker crust
1½ quarts coffee ice cream
Shaved chocolate

Spread fudge sauce over bottom of crust.
Fill crust with softened ice cream. Sprinkle
with shaved chocolate. Freeze and enjoy!

"Mmmm! It sounds delicious!" I say to
Mom when I'm done reading. "But there's
something I don't get. How did you know I
was going to make an A+ on my test?"

Mom smiles. "With all the studying you
did, I had a feeling you would do well."

I smile. "I can't wait to try the pie. All
the ingredients sound like they'll taste
really good together."

Mom smiles and nods her head like she agrees. "I think that's why they call it A+ Ice Cream Pie. Sometimes things add up just right."

I smile back. Mom is right. Sometimes things do add up just right, and when they do, it is an A+ feeling.

THE SWEET SMELL OF SUCCESS

Strawberry-scented dog shampoo.
Check.
Bucket and brush.
Check. Check.
Soap. Powder. Perfume.
Check. Check. Check.
Now that I've taken care of my boy
problem and my dad problem, I just need to

take care of two more problems: my brother problem and his smelly dog problem.

My brother problem actually sort of took care of itself. Ever since I have been in trouble with Mom and Dad, Max has been a whole lot nicer to me. I want to do something nice for him.

Now all I have to do is to wait for him to get home from baseball practice. When he does, I tell him to close his eyes. "I have a big surprise for you," I say.

"I hope it's fresh out of the oven and has nuts and chocolate chips in it," says Max.

"Um, not exactly," I tell my brother as I lead him back to our bathroom. When we get there, I tell him to open his eyes.

He looks around the bathroom like he's not sure what he's looking at, so I explain. "We have everything we need to give Champ a bath," I say to Max.

Max looks down at the pile of bottles and boxes and the stack of towels next to the tub. "This is a surprise. But I'm not sure it's a good one. Can't we give Champ a bath another day?"

I hold my nose like I've had enough smelly dog. "No way," I tell my brother. I turn on the water and add some shampoo. The tub starts filling up with bubbles.

"It looks like my dog is about to get the bath of his life," Max says with a smile.

I turn the water off. "All we need now is the dog."

Max goes to get Champ. He takes Champ's collar off, and Champ jumps right in. He barks and splashes around like he's a toddler in a baby pool. When he does, water and bubbles go everywhere. I look at Max and laugh. We both look like we're taking baths too.

"I think he likes it," says Max.

"He smells better already," I say. I pick up a shampoo bottle and squirt shampoo all over Champ's head and back. Max and I work together to lather and scrub.

When Champ is all soapy, Max holds him while I pour water over him and rinse him off.

Champ shakes off the water, and our clothes aren't the only things that are wet. "The bathroom looks like it took a bath," I say.

Max grabs some towels and tosses me one. "I'll dry off Champ while you dry off the sink and mirror. If Mom comes in here, we're toast."

We work together until everything in the bathroom, including Champ, is clean and dry. When we're done, I squirt Champ with a few sprays of doggie perfume. He smells so good,

I squirt him with a few more. Then I take a deep breath. If you ask me, Champ has never smelled better. "You smell so good, I don't even mind if you sleep on my bed."

Champ licks me like he's glad I'm happy.

"You're a good boy," I say to Champ.

Max pats him. "Thanks," says Max with a smile.

I laugh. He knows I wasn't talking about him, but the truth is, he's being good too. It's nice doing something fun with my brother. And it's a whole lot better than arguing about something I did that embarrassed him.

"Giving Champ a bath was a good idea," Max says like he can read my mind.

I snap my fingers. "I have another good idea. Meet me in front of the TV. You bring the dog, and I'll bring the cookies. Mom and I baked some this morning."

Max nods like he approves.

I knew he would. My brother never says no to food.

I run to the kitchen and grab the tray of cookies Mom and I made. They look a whole lot better than the ones I made last weekend. When I get to the den, Max and Champ are already there with the TV on. Max even has a show on that we both like.

I plop down on the couch next to them. Max takes a handful of cookies from the tray.

"Mmmm!" he says between bites.

I smile. I think Max and I are officially having a nice brother-sister moment.

I look down at the tray of cookies on the coffee table and think about the cookies I made for JT. I can't help frowning. I didn't think the boy I would be sharing cookies with would be my brother.

Max swallows his mouthful of cookies, and then he gets a look on his face like he can tell what's on my mind. "Hey Mal, I've been doing some thinking about this whole JT thing. Can I give you some big-brotherly advice?"

I nod. This is the first time in the history of my life that Max has given me big-brotherly advice about anything, and I can't wait to hear what it is.

Max gives me the same serious look Dad gives me when he wants to make sure I'm listening. "The next time you like a boy, I think you should stick to one you know and, even better, stick to one your own age."

I think about what Max said. I definitely agree with him about getting to know someone before you decide if you like that person. And I know why Max wants me to like someone my own age. He doesn't want me to embarrass him in front of his friends.

But here's what Max doesn't know.

"There won't be a next time," I tell my brother.

I think about the promise I made to Mom and Dad and Mr. Knight that I wouldn't let anything get in the way of my schoolwork, and I'm not going to.

"I'm done with boys," I tell my brother. "I have more important things to think about."

Max laughs. "I'm sure you do. I'm also sure there will be more boys in your future. I just hope it isn't anytime soon."

I hold up my pinkie and look at Max. "Let's pinkie swear that it won't be anytime soon."

Max groans, grabs another handful of cookies, and gives me a *he-wouldn't-pinkie-swear-if-it-were-the-only-thing-left-to-do* look.

Then he shakes his head and changes the channel to the baseball game.

I smile and take a cookie from the tray. It was nice while it lasted, but I think my brother-sister moment with Max is officially over.

HAPPILY EVER AFTER

Since I don't like watching baseball, I go to my room and get out a sheet of paper.

Mr. Knight tells us that when important things happen, we should write about them. Since a lot of important things have happened in my life lately, now seems like a good time to do some writing.

I take out my favorite purple glitter pen and get started.

HAPPILY EVER AFTER
A Short Story with a Catchy Cartoon
By Mallory McDonald

Once upon a time, there lived a smart, sweet, cute, fashionable girl (see illustration on next page).

Even though this girl was not only smart, sweet, cute, fashionable but also good at math, baking cookies (with her mom's help), and washing dogs, for a while, things didn't seem to go her way.

A bunch of bad things happened. Blah. Blah. Blah.

She got in trouble (with her teacher and her parents). Plus, her brother was mad at her. More blah, blah, blah.

But who likes reading blah, blah, blah? So let's just skip to the happy ending. Ta-Da! Here it is!

P.C.A.N.J.A.T.H.M.
(pretty cute and not just according to her mother)

100% pure sweet

Her outfit

Fashion Fran certified cute

Everyone in the story got over their madness (I'm talking about the girl's teacher and her parents and her brother). They all told her how smart, sweet, cute, and fashionable she was. (They didn't actually tell her this, but she could tell they were thinking it.) Everybody except the guy she had a crush on, but she didn't care. She barely knew him anyway.

And the girl lived happily ever after with her cat, Cheeseburger.

THE END

Except for the catchy cartoon.

C.B.a.C.W.I.M

(Short for: C below a C what I mean.)

MALLORY'S INBOX

Max is watching baseball.

Mom is drinking coffee.

Dad is reading a book.

Champ is asleep next to Cheeseburger.
I pat them both on their heads. Champ
doesn't even open his eyes. I think his bath
made him tired.

I go into the kitchen to check my email.
I'm glad I do because my inbox is jam-
packed!

Subject: Your F.C.
From: chatterbox
To: malgal

Hi Mallory,
Guess what...your F.C. (short for *former crush*) is at my house. He and Bailey came over to watch TV and eat popcorn with Winnie. And guess what else . . . you should be glad you're not here watching TV and eating popcorn with him. He snorts when he laughs and he tells stupid jokes and he chews with his mouth open. Gross! Gross! Gross! I bet that makes you glad he is your F.C. and not your C.C. (short for *current crush*). It makes me glad for you.

Your C.A.A.L.B.F.F. (*Short for current and always lifelong best friend forever*),
Mary Ann

Subject: One more thing
From: chatterbox
To: malgal

Mallory,
One more thing. I AM COMING OVER TO YOUR HOUSE!
I can't even watch *Fashion Fran* because Winnie says she and Bailey "*need*" the TV and that they were here first. So can you please get the popcorn ready? (I guess that is two things.)
Mary Ann

Subject: Study Date
From: smartiegirl
To: malgal
Hi Mallory,
Congrats on making an A+ on your math

test. As you and Mary Ann would say, "Wow! Wow! Wow!" Do you mind if I copy you and Mary Ann? Also, do you want to come over next Saturday and study for the next test?
    Say yes!
    Pamela

Subject: Proud of you!
From: maxandmallory'sdad
To: malgal

Mallory,
    Mom and I just wanted to tell you again how proud we are of your grade on your math test. Stay focused (that means eyes on your textbook), and keep up the good work.
    We love you!
    Mom and Dad

A GUIDEBOOK
FROM MALLORY

Welcome to my guidebook on boys, brothers, dads, and dogs. Lately, I've learned a lot about all of these topics. Even though I'm sure my dad, my brother, boys everywhere, and dogs (if they could talk) would say I still have a lot to learn, I hope my tips, tricks, and wisdom are helpful. Have fun reading!

BOYS

I will admit I still don't know a lot about this topic, but here is what I do know: If you think you like a boy, it is probably best to get to know him first and then decide if you like him. And if you think it is a good idea to bake cookies for him and take them to his house, THINK AGAIN! Go ahead and bake the cookies (with some help) and eat them yourself. Better yet, call some friends to come over and eat them with you.

BROTHERS

Here are some DOS and DON'TS for getting along with brothers.

DO try to be nice to them, and they will (hopefully) be nice to you.

DON'T embarrass them. If you do, I'm pretty sure they won't be so nice.

DO bake cookies for them. Brothers love cookies.

IMPORTANT NOTE: These DOS and DON'TS are for older brothers because that is the kind that I have. I think some of them will probably work for younger brothers (and maybe sisters) too.

DADS

There is a simple trick to get along with dads. DO YOUR SCHOOLWORK. Maybe there are some other tricks to getting along with dads (and moms and teachers), but I know for sure this one works.

DOGS

I actually have a few tips to share about dogs.

Tip #1: Buy some shampoo and dog perfume. Trust me, you'll be glad you did.

Tip #2: Don't be afraid to give your dog a bath. It can be a little messy, but when the scent of fresh, clean dog fills the room, you will know it was worth it.

Tip #3: If a clean dog decides to make himself at home on your bed, enjoy every minute of it.

I hope my guidebook was helpful. When it comes to boys, brothers, dads, and dogs, I'm sure you'll come up with plenty of ways to handle them on your own.

That's it for now.
Big, huge hugs and kisses!
Mallory

Darby Creek
A division of Lerner Publishing Group, Inc.
241 First Avenue North
Minneapolis, MN 55401 U.S.A.

Website address: www.lernerbooks.com

FSC

Mixed Sources
Product group from well-managed forests, controlled sources and recycled wood or fiber

Cert no. BV-COC-930557
www.fsc.org
© 1996 Forest Stewardship Council

Library of Congress Cataloging-in-Publication Data

Friedman, Laurie B.
    Mallory's guide to boys, brothers, dads, and dogs / by Laurie Friedman ; illustrations by Jennifer Kalis.
        p.   cm. — (Mallory ; #15)
    Summary: Ten-year-old Mallory's crush on JT, a boy in her older brother's class, gets her in trouble with her teacher, her family, and her friends but no matter what she does, JT does not seem interested in her.
    ISBN: 978-0-8225-8886-3 (trade hard cover : alk. paper)
    [1. Interpersonal relations—Fiction. 2. Schools—Fiction. 3. Family life—Fiction. 4. Dogs—Fiction.] I. Kalis, Jennifer, ill. II. Title.
    PZ7.F89773Mar 2011
    [Fic]—dc22   2010022224

Manufactured in the United States of America
1 — BP — 12/31/10